SNAKES SET II

COMMON ADDERS

Adam G. Klein
ABDO Publishing Company

visit us at
www.abdopub.com

Published by ABDO Publishing Company, 4940 Viking Drive, Edina, Minnesota 55435.
Copyright © 2006 by Abdo Consulting Group, Inc. International copyrights reserved in all countries. No part of this book may be reproduced in any form without written permission from the publisher. The Checkerboard Library™ is a trademark and logo of ABDO Publishing Company.

Printed in the United States.

Cover Photo: Corbis
Interior Photos: Animals Animals pp. 7, 17, 19; Corbis pp. 5, 9, 10, 15, 21; Peter Arnold p. 11

Series Coordinator: Megan Murphy
Editors: Stephanie Hedlund, Megan Murphy
Art Direction & Maps: Neil Klinepier

Library of Congress Cataloging-in-Publication Data

Klein, Adam G., 1976-
   Common adders / Adam G. Klein.
      p. cm. -- (Snakes. Set II)
   ISBN 1-59679-279-5
      1. Vipera berus--Juvenile literature. I. Title.

 QL666.O69K53 2005
 597.96'36--dc22
                                                         2005043332

CONTENTS

Common Adders

In northern Europe, hundreds of snakes hide together underground. It has been about six months since they last saw the sun. The snakes are patiently waiting for winter to end. As soon as it gets warm, they will slither out into the world again.

These snakes are *Vipera berus*, or common adders. They are also known as the European viper or northern adder. They are found farther north in Europe than any other snake.

The common adder belongs to the Viperidae **family**. Vipers have a pair of long, hollow fangs attached to movable bones on the upper jaw. These fangs can be folded back in the mouth when not in use.

Snakes are reptiles, which are vertebrates. This means they have a backbone just like a human. Unlike humans, snakes are cold-blooded creatures. They rely on outside heat sources to maintain their body temperature.

Adders are protected by law, so it is illegal for humans to kill them.

SIZES

Common adders have stout bodies. Their narrow heads end with a blunt snout. Their eyes have a **vertical** pupil, like a cat's eyes. This feature is common in **nocturnal** animals. The vertical pupil helps to limit the amount of light coming into the eye.

Adult common adders are usually between 19 and 24 inches (48 and 61 cm) long. Female common adders grow much larger than males. It is easy to tell them apart in the wild. The largest females can be 34 inches (86 cm) long.

All snakes have scales for skin. Common adders shed their skin several times a year. Shedding occurs when a snake has outgrown its skin. Male common adders also shed when they are ready to mate.

The vertical pupils of the common adder help it see better at night.

COLORS

Common adders can usually be identified by the markings on their bodies. Scales on the adder's head form an X or **chevron** mark. Traveling down the back of the common adder is a dark zigzag pattern. Sometimes, this pattern has black spots on the side.

Gray, brown, olive, and yellow are common colors for the adder. They can sometimes be red, too. Females are darker than the male adders. But, the colors on the males contrast each other more than on the females.

The adder's primarily dark colors help it stay warm in its cold **environment**. In fact, some adders are completely black. They usually live the farthest north. Dark colors absorb more heat from the sun. So, their black color helps them warm up more quickly.

Opposite page: *Only a small percentage of adders are completely black. The disadvantage of this color is that black adders are not as camouflaged as snakes with the zigzag markings.*

WHERE THEY LIVE

The common adder lives in many types of **habitats**. They like scrubland, rocky hillsides, and meadowy woods. Some populations live on high mountains or in the Arctic **tundra**. Common adders are able to survive in some of the coldest places in the world.

Adders typically live together in dens during the winter. They also gather during the breeding season.

The best time to see common adders is in early spring when they emerge from hibernation.

Common adders live in group dens in the winter. They make their nests in tree stumps, under roots, or in animal burrows. In the spring, the male adders leave the dens to find warm, open places to sun themselves. A few weeks later, the females join them.

As summer approaches, the adders split into smaller groups to look for food. They sleep during the day when it gets too hot and travel during the night.

WHERE THEY ARE FOUND

The common adder has a fitting name. This snake is the most widely distributed snake in northern Europe, including Scandinavia. Their **habitat** continues across Russia and northern China, all the way to the Pacific Ocean.

Common adders are the only poisonous snake in northern Europe. They are also the only snake species that can be found in the Arctic Circle.

Common adders survive through the winter by hibernating. Hibernation is like a long sleep. The length of the hibernation depends on how far north the snake is. Closer to the North Pole, common adders are only active for three to four months each year.

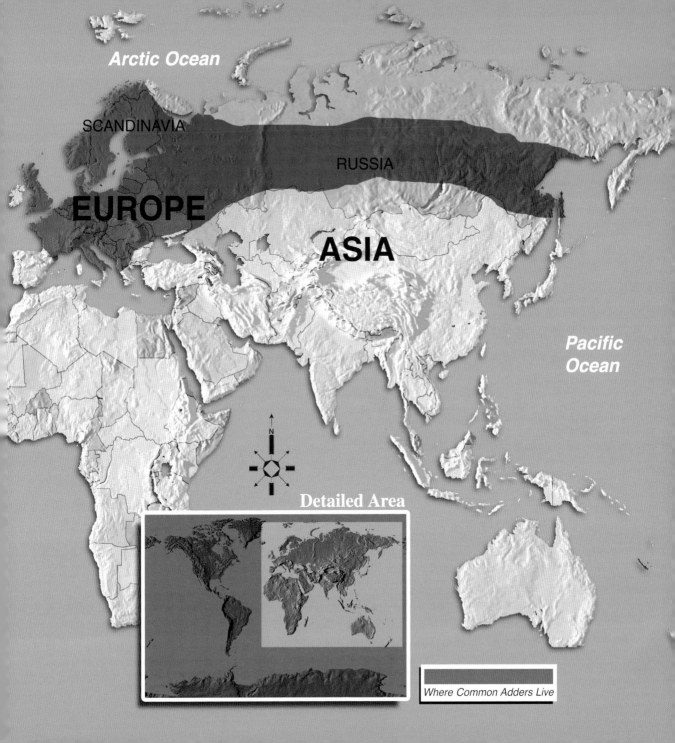

Arctic Ocean

SCANDINAVIA

RUSSIA

EUROPE

ASIA

Pacific Ocean

N

Detailed Area

Where Common Adders Live

SENSES

Like all snakes, common adders have very poor vision. They also don't have ears. So, they must rely on other senses to help them survive. These senses are more highly developed than a human's.

Snakes have a very keen sense of smell. They use their tongue to pick up scent particles and then deposit them in their mouth. Then, a special receptor called the Jacobson's organ identifies the particles. This receptor helps the snake figure out what is nearby.

Snakes also use vibrations to sense motion. A bone in their lower jaw helps them detect movement. They keep their heads low to the ground when they move. This way, they can tell if there is food or a **predator** nearby.

Opposite page: *Unlike most other snakes, adders have a considerable tolerance for cold weather. They are often found in dry, open, sunny places when they are not hibernating.*

DEFENSE

Few creatures try to eat the common adder. Most animals avoid poisonous creatures. However, young adders are often killed by buzzards or adult snakes. And, **rodents** will sometimes eat hibernating adders.

When threatened, the adder hisses loudly and continuously before attacking. Adders strike quickly and repeatedly if cornered or alarmed. Common adders have enough **venom** to kill small creatures, but usually not humans.

Still, they are very dangerous and should be respected at all times. If bitten by a common adder, a person should immediately go to a hospital. But as long as the snakes are not threatened, they should not attack.

The biggest challenge to the common adder's survival is its **environment**. Death from overheating, freezing, or **dehydration** is common.

The common adder is usually a shy snake. But, it will strike if it feels threatened.

FOOD

Common adders hibernate and go without food all winter. So when they are active during the summer, they need to eat a lot. Common adders will eat eggs, lizards, frogs, and small mammals.

Their **venom** is used for defending themselves and killing prey. When hunting, adders strike quickly. They **inject** a deadly amount of poison into their prey. Then, they wait for the animal to die.

Like all snakes, adders swallow their prey whole. Their jaws are designed to unhinge so they can eat animals much larger than their head. Also, their ribs are not joined. That way, their bodies can expand as their meal moves through their system.

The adder has very powerful **digestive** fluids. Most of the prey will be absorbed completely. Only the hair and teeth pass through.

This common adder is ready to eat its next meal.

BABIES

The spring mating season lasts about four weeks. Two male common adders will compete with each other for a female. To do this, they **intertwine** the front parts of their bodies and try to wrestle each other to the ground.

The victor mates with the female immediately. The other adder retreats to the side where it patiently waits until it can sneak back. After they mate, females seek out a suitable place to give birth. They will often travel more than half a mile (1 km) from their hibernation site.

Common adders do not lay their eggs like many other snakes. Instead, the eggs stay inside the mother snake. She carries and protects them until they are fully developed. The eggs hatch while still inside of her.

Within two months of mating, the baby snakes are born. This is usually the end of summer. Most common adders give birth every year. However in the extreme north, mother adders only give birth every other year.

The brood will contain between 6 and 20 new snakes. Each baby will be about six to nine inches (15 to 23 cm) long.

In the spring, male adders will fight for mating rights. People often mistake two intertwined male adders as a mating pair.

Adders can live up to 20 years in the wild. Their survival often depends on the severity of the weather in the winter.

GLOSSARY

chevron - a figure or pattern in the shape of a V or an upside-down V.

dehydration (dee-heye-DRAY-shun) - the result of too little water. A person or animal becomes dehydrated when the fluid used and lost is not replaced.

digest - to break down food into substances small enough for the body to absorb.

environment - all the surroundings that affect the growth and well-being of a living thing.

family - a group that scientists use to classify similar plants or animals. It ranks above a genus and below an order.

habitat - a place where a living thing is naturally found.

inject - to forcefully introduce a fluid into the body, usually with a needle or something sharp.

intertwine - to wrap two or more things around each other.

nocturnal (nahk-TUHR-nuhl) - active at night.

predator - an animal that kills and eats other animals.

rodent - any of several related animals that have large front teeth for gnawing.

tundra - a vast, treeless plain in the Arctic. The ground beneath its surface is frozen all year long.

venom - a poison produced by some animals and insects. It usually enters a victim through a bite or sting.

vertical - in the up-and-down position.

WEB SITES

To learn more about common adders, visit ABDO Publishing Company on the World Wide Web at **www.abdopub.com**. Web sites about these snakes are featured on our Book Links page. These links are routinely monitored and updated to provide the most current information available.

INDEX